Tali

CW00854262

Foreword

These stories were made up as bedtime tales for my new grandson.

Thanks to 'Uncle Donald' for coming up with the name 'Tali'.

Thanks also to William McGonagall, Dixon Lanier Merritt, William Hughes Mearns and Spike Milligan for their contributions to the 'Poetry' section.

Another batch of wonderful illustrations from Anne Hulse; and two from her granddaughters, Evie and Lilly (see if you can spot them).

Some of these stories contain characters from my other books of bedtime stories:

- *The Rabbit with Three Ears*
- *Martha, the Magical Mouse*
- *Misha Supercat*

GJ Abercrombie

Edinburgh

2019

For my grandchildren

Chapter 1

Meet Tali

Tali is a hound.

A hound is a kind of dog that has a very clever nose; it is good at sniffing things out.

Tali loves books. He is a bookhound.

He loves books so much that he owns his own library! The library is in an old converted camper-van, which he calls 'Esmerelda'. Esmerelda has a small cooking stove for making cups of tea or coffee and a little sink for washing the cups afterwards. There is a toaster for heating emergency snacks and a desk where Tali sits to serve his customers.

Every other space is taken up with books.

Books are everywhere!

There are so many books that there is no room for Tali's bed in the van. It is up in a little tent on the roof.

Tali drives the mobile library from place to place lending books to anyone who wants one. You know that when you are sick you go to the doctor's? The doctor gives you medicine to make you better. Well, people who have worries or problems can visit Tali's library and he will find a book to help them. Tali loves to hear how the books have helped the people who borrowed them.

Each morning, Tali arrives in a new town or village and parks the library near the playpark or the school. He always tries to make it easy for the people who live there to find him. He toots Esmerelda's horn to let people know that he has arrived and they come to visit him, bringing the books they have already borrowed back with them.

There are three ways of choosing a book in Tali's library:

1. Sometimes, the person chooses the book …

   If people already know which book they want to borrow from the library, they can go straight to the shelf and select it.

2. Sometimes, the book chooses the person! …

   Some people are not too sure exactly which book they want. As long as they know roughly what type of book they want to read, they can look in the correct section of the library: funny books, cooking books, travel books …

   The books themselves also seem to know what each person is looking for. If a particular book thinks that a person would like to read it, it edges itself out a little bit from all the other books on the shelf. The customer notices the book sticking out and takes it.

3. Sometimes, Tali chooses the book for the person …

   A lot of people just simply don't know what kind of book they want.

This is where Tali's clever nose helps. He sits at his desk and chats with the customer, maybe with a cup of tea or a glass of water. He asks them about their lives; what they like, what they don't like. He gets them to talk about their worries or problems and his nose 'sniffs out' the ideal book for them.

When they have finished chatting and his nose starts twitching, Tali opens up the top-left drawer of his desk and there, magically, is the perfect book for that person!

Each person is allowed to borrow as many books as they like but they must return them the next time Tali's library-van comes to their town.

When he first started his library, Tali wanted to encourage people to read books. His 'good idea' was to put a bar of chocolate inside every book. He told the people to eat one piece every time they finished a chapter and bring the book back when the chocolate was all done.

One naughty girl came back the same day saying that she had finished reading the whole book. "I'd like another bar of chocolate … I mean … another book", she said.

She had chocolate all over her face.

When Tali asked her about what had happened in the story, she could not answer any of his questions.

She had not read the book at all!

She had just eaten all the chocolate and wanted some more! *(Cheeky!)*

Tali soon discovered that people do not need chocolate to encourage them to read; all they need is for the books to be interesting or helpful.

When Tali helps people, they often give him a present to thank him. If they ask what he would like, he usually asks for a small fridge-magnet. He sticks these to the side of his desk to remind him of all the fun he has had with his friends in the library-van.

Each night, all of the books which people have brought back to the library arrange themselves into a big pile on the floor of the van.

They form a staircase which Tali uses to climb up to his bed in the roof.

During the night, while Tali is asleep, the books all go back to their correct places on the shelves, ready for the next day's business.

All by themselves! They are magical books!

Chapter 2

Baby Books

Each morning, when Tali wakes up, the books have all filed themselves away onto the shelves. There is no longer a staircase to help him get down from the roof.

He has to 'dreep' down. 'Dreep' is a good Scottish word.

It means that he has to lower himself as far as his arms will reach, dangle by his fingers and let himself fall the rest of the way to the floor of the van. He does not mind doing this because at least it means that he does not have to put all the books back onto the shelves.

Some mornings, he buys his breakfast in a café and other times he just has a cup of tea in the library-van. Then he sets off to his next village. Some of the places he visits already have a library but people still like to visit Tali's van because his books seem to be a bit different …

… as we shall hear!

One day, a lady called Mrs Black came into the van, looking very worried.

Tali asked her what was wrong and she said,

"Oh, Mr Bookhound, I'm so sorry but something dreadful has happened to one of your books."

"First of all", he said, "please call me 'Tali'. Everyone does."

"That's a nice name. Where does it come from?" she asked.

"It's short for 'Talisker'. Now tell me about the book. What happened?"

"I was reading my baby, Mary-Anna, a story and she liked the pictures so much that she reached out and grabbed it. She has ripped the page in half."

(Can you see which book it was? ...

... That's right ... it was The Rabbit with Three Ears!)

Tali said that she should not worry. He said he could repair it with some sticky tape.

He sat down at his desk and thought about a book suitable for Mary-Anna.

His nose twitched and suddenly there was a brilliant flash inside the top-left drawer of this desk. Tali could see the bright light shining out from the cracks around the drawer. Mrs Black could not see the flash as she was sitting at the other side of the desk.

Tali opened the drawer and there he found a book with strong pages made of cardboard.

"These books are specially designed for babies", he said, "They can't tear the thick pages."

"Oh thanks. That's great", she said and off she went with Mary-Anna in her pram.

A little while later, she returned looking even more worried.

"What's wrong now?" asked Tali.

She said, "I'm so sorry but I think I've ruined another one of your books".

She took a squishy lump of black cardboard out of her bag and put it on Tali's desk.

"Yuk! What's that?" cried Tali.

"It's your book!" said Mrs Black.

"But it's all squishy", he replied.

"Mary-Anna was enjoying the pictures so much that she would not put it down. She took it into the bath with her and then she dropped it into the water", she explained.

"And how did it get all black?" Tali asked her.

"I tried to dry it with my hair-dryer but that did not work, so I put it into the toaster in my kitchen and it seems to have caught fire", she wailed.

"You should never put anything except bread or hot-cross-buns (HCBs) into a toaster", said Tali.

"I know that now!" wailed Mrs Black.

"Don't worry", said Tali, feeling sorry for her as he thought about the problem of taking books into the bath.

His nose twitched and there was another flash of light at his desk.

Tali opened the special drawer again and said:

"Here, try this book".

He gave her a special plastic book which is designed so that babies can take them into the bath. The book was called *'Splish Splash'* and it had a picture of a fish on its cover.

Mrs Black thanked Tali and said that she would try to make sure that this book did not get damaged like the others.

Mary-Anna seemed pleased with the new book and immediately put it in her mouth and started to bite it with her teeth.

Her mummy told her not to eat the book and said "Sorry" to Tali again!

Tali just smiled and told her not to worry.

When Mrs Black had gone away, Tali looked at the side of his desk.

He noticed that a new fridge-magnet had appeared all by itself.

The magnet was in the shape of a rubber duck.

It reminded Tali of the bath-book he had given to Mary-Anna and he wondered how she would manage to ruin THAT book too!

Tali wondered what to have for his tea that night and then he remembered telling Mary-Anna's mum about the toaster earlier on.

(Do you remember what Tali said were the only two things you should put in a toaster? ...

... That's right: Bread and Hot-Cross-Buns (HCBs)

Tali bought himself two HCBs from the shop.

He heated them in his own toaster and spread a little butter on them.

They were YUMMY!

Chapter 3

Travel Books

One day, Tali drove Esmerelda to their usual spot in a little village in Fife, called 'Star'. 'Star' is a lovely name for a lovely little village.

It was just after breakfast time but there was already someone waiting for the library-van to arrive. It was his friend Lewis Watson.

"Good morning, Lewis", said Tali, "You're up early today".

"Oh, I had to get here early because I'm so busy at work. I need to be in my office by 8 o'clock every morning", he replied, looking at his watch.

"You look very tired", said Tali, "Come in and tell me what the problem is." They both sat at his desk in the library-van and Lewis told Tali how he was exhausted. He was working too hard and never got any proper sleep.

"It sounds like you need a holiday", said the bookhound with a smile.

"Oh, I haven't had a holiday for years", came the reply.

"Let's see if I can help", said Tali. "If you did have a holiday, where would you like to go?"

Lewis had a look at the 'TRAVEL' section of the library and chose a book about the North Pole.

"That sounds exciting!" said Lewis, "Let's a have a look at this book".

"We can do a lot more than just <u>look</u> at these books", said Tali with a grin.

He placed the magic book in a special stand on top of his desk and opened it up. As soon as the book was opened, the door of the library-van closed all by itself. Then, something strange happened. All of the books on the shelves started to move round to the left.

Soon the whole library seemed to be spinning around with Tali and Lewis inside.

Just as suddenly, it stopped spinning and the door of the van opened again.

There was an icy blast and a big flurry of snow blew into the library. They were actually there; at the North Pole!

They carefully stepped out of the van making sure not to slip on the icy snow on the ground.

"BBBRRRRR, it's freezing here", said Lewis. He was only wearing shorts and a t-shirt because it had been warm and sunny in his village back home.

Suddenly, a huge polar bear appeared and ran towards them; growling. It looked very angry and very hungry so Tali and Lewis ran back into the van. The polar bear chased them all the way.

Tali found the tuna sandwich he was going to eat for his lunch and threw it out of the door. The bear gobbled it up in one bite and came looking for more. It was about to stick its head inside the van so Tali quickly slammed the door shut.

"Phew! That was close", Tali said, "Maybe we should try somewhere else for your holiday".

Lewis found another book on the shelf and gave it to Tali, saying "I've always wanted to go to America." Tali placed it on the book-stand and when he opened it, the books in the van started spinning around again.

This time, when the books stopped spinning and Tali opened the door, the noise was deafening.

The library-van was sitting in the middle of a road junction in the heart of New York City!

There were lots of cars and buses and yellow taxicabs, all tooting their horns because the van was blocking the road. A big policeman was blowing his whistle angrily and waving his arms about. He started to walk over towards the van and was taking some handcuffs from his tool-belt.

"Oh-Oh", said Tali and quickly closed the door again.

"New York is not a very relaxing holiday place", said Lewis as he speedily selected a book about Spain from the shelf. "Try this one", he said to Tali, "It's got a picture of a beach on it. I remember going to the seaside and playing on the beach when I was a small boy."

When Tali opened this book on the stand, the shelves started spinning for a third time. When they stopped and the door opened, there was a blast of heat from outside.

The sun was shining and the van was parked beside a lovely sandy beach. There were lots of people sitting on deckchairs or lying on towels. Groups of happy children were splashing in the sea.

It was so hot that Tali and Lewis had some lemonade to drink.

There was a sudden crash and a plastic frisbee came flying in the door of the van. It hit Lewis's cup and splashed his drink all over his face.

Two boys appeared at the door and said, "Oopsee! Sorry! There's no room for us to play on the beach".

Spain was very nice but just a bit too busy for Lewis. "Look at all the crowds", he sighed, "I'm not sure I want that".

Tali sat at his desk and asked Lewis what kind of holiday he would REALLY like.

Lewis replied, "When I was a boy I remember looking forward to holidays with my family. We had ice-cream at lunch-time and if it was windy we would fly a kite on the beach. On our way home, we would always buy fish and chips and eat them in the car."

Tali's nose twitched a bit. It had 'sniffed out' the perfect holiday for Lewis.

There was a flash in the drawer of Tali's desk and when he opened it, there was a book about Scotland.

Tali placed it on the book-stand and opened it in the middle.

When the spinning stopped and the door of the van opened, they were parked beside the harbour at North Berwick.

They spent the day playing Crazy-Golf and flying a kite on the beach. They had ice-cream at lunchtime. Lewis bought a cuddly octopus toy in a shop to remind himself of his great holiday.

He said that he felt much happier after his relaxing holiday and they both agreed that you don't have to travel far to have a break from work.

When it was time to go home, Tali offered to use the library-van's spinning technique.

"You just close the book on the stand and the book-shelves spin round the other way to take you home", he explained to Lewis.

"I think it would be nicer if we just drove back", said Lewis, "That way we can stop for fish and chips on the way. I'd like to buy them for you to thank you for my lovely holiday".

So, that's what happened. Lewis bought fish and chips for Tali and a haggis and chips for himself. They ate them out of newspapers in the library-van looking out over the sea.

Delicious!

Just before going up to his bed that night, Tali noticed a new magnet on the side of his desk.

It was in the shape of an octopus … eating chips.

Chapter 4

Music Books

Tali parked his library-van, Esmerelda, on the promenade in Portobello. He bought himself a tasty bagel from a café on the corner and sat on the steps of the van to have his breakfast.

Along came his first customer of the day. It was someone he knew very well.

Her name is Mrs O'Hare and she had brought him some carrots from her garden.

As you may know, Mrs O'Hare is the leader of the Dancing Rabbit Chorus which is based in Portobello. This is a group of rabbit friends who sing and dance to entertain people.

"How are you today, Mrs No-hair … sorry … Mrs O'Hare?" asked Tali.

The kind rabbit just laughed and said, "Don't worry. I know the other rabbits call me that. I don't really mind."

"Well then, how can I help you today?" asked the bookhound as he wiped the bagel crumbs from his mouth.

"I'm looking for some new music for the chorus", she said, "We're all a bit fed up singing the same songs over and over again. But, I don't know exactly what type of music I'm looking for".

"Then you've come to the right place", said Tali with a knowing smile.

"Have a look in the 'MUSIC' section of the library and see if anything 'pops out' for you", he added.

Mrs O'Hare went into the library-van and found a shelf marked 'MUSIC' near the back. She walked along looking at all the books. She was amazed at all the different types of music there were.

There were books on:

- Classical Music
  - Not really what the rabbits like, she thought
- Rap Music
  - Not really what SHE likes
- Heavy Metal Music
  - Not very easy to dance to
- Big Band Music
  - Not many words in these tunes
- Barbershop Music
  - Usually sung by all-men or all-women groups. Hers is an 'all-rabbit' group

Mrs O'Hare was finding it hard to choose when suddenly she felt something poking at her arm. She looked down and saw that a book was sticking out from the shelf. It was gently nudging her elbow as if to say, "Look at me!"

Mrs O'Hare pulled the book out from beside its neighbours on the shelf and saw that it was called:

Music from Dixie

The title was written in RED and BLUE letters on a **WHITE** background; the same colours as the American flag. Dixie is an old name for the southern part of the United States of America.

Mrs O'Hare took it over to Tali at his desk and he said, "Let's see if we can find something you like in here".

He placed the magic book on the magic book-stand and opened it at a chapter called:

New Orleans

The door of the van closed itself and the books began to whirl around. Mrs O'Hare was feeling a bit dizzy so she held onto Tali's desk until it all stopped spinning.

Then the door opened and they heard some wonderful music. The library-van was in the middle of a large park. There were lots of people listening and dancing to the band playing.

It was very lively!

"I love Jazz", said Mrs O'Hare and she got up to leave the van.

"Hang on a minute", said Tali, "You might need this" and he handed her a frilly fan. She took the fan, leapt out of the library-van and joined in with the dancing.

Then the man playing the trumpet came down from the stage and walked right out of the park gates. He was still playing, so everyone danced along behind him.

They went right down the middle of the main street and all the people came out of their houses and shops to join in.

The whole street seemed to come alive with music and dancing.

Soon Mrs O'Hare was tired and wanted to sit down. She and Tali went into a café to buy some lemonade. She was wiping her face with a handkerchief and wafting herself with the fan that Tali had given her.

In the corner of the café, there were some more people playing music. This was much quieter and more relaxed than the Jazz music they had heard before.

It was called 'Blues Music' and Tali and Mrs O'Hare tapped their feet gently along to the rhythm. Some people got up to dance but the two travellers just sat and watched.

When the music stopped, they finished their lemonade and made their way back to the library-van.

Tali opened the Dixie Music book at a chapter called:

Nashville

The books spun around and around and Mrs O'Hare felt dizzy again.

When it stopped, she found she was wearing a 'cow-girl' outfit. She had on high leather boots with metal studs, a fringed waistcoat and a Stetson hat.

"Let's go hear some good ol' Country Music. YEE-HAH", she shouted in a weird 'American' accent as they stepped down from the van.

Everywhere they went, they saw people playing guitars and singing songs.

They joined in a group who were line-dancing. This involves great concentration. You have to do the same steps and claps as everyone around you ... and at the same time too!

"I'm not sure if the Dancing Rabbit Chorus could manage this", she said to Tali, "but we'd have great fun trying!"

Later, they returned to the van so that they could sit down for a rest.

Tali opened the book at another chapter called:

Memphis

When they opened the door pf the van, they saw that they were in the car-park of the 'Memphis Music Hall of Fame'. This is an amazing museum where there are photographs of lots of famous musicians who played all kinds of different music:

- Rock 'n' Roll
- Pop
- Bluegrass
- Soul
- As well as the three she had already heard on her trip ...
    - *Do you remember what they were?*
        - *Jazz Music*
        - *Blues Music*
        - *Country Music*

They had a good look at the museum and then it was time to leave. Just before they went back to the library-van, Mrs O'Hare went into the gift-shop at the museum.

(I wonder what she bought, do you?)

"There are so many different types of music. I don't know which to choose for the chorus", said Mrs O'Hare when the books stopped spinning and they were back in Portobello.

"Then let me help", said Tali, "That's what I'm here for".

There was a secret flash in his top-left drawer and Tali opened it and took out a big, thick book called:

100 Songs from Around the World

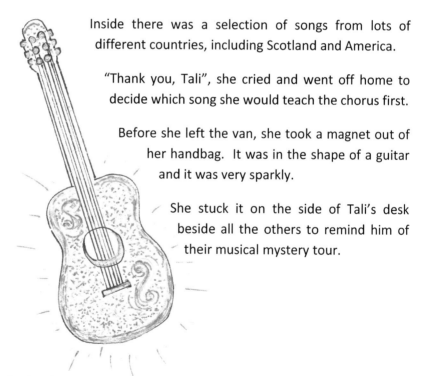

Inside there was a selection of songs from lots of different countries, including Scotland and America.

"Thank you, Tali", she cried and went off home to decide which song she would teach the chorus first.

Before she left the van, she took a magnet out of her handbag. It was in the shape of a guitar and it was very sparkly.

She stuck it on the side of Tali's desk beside all the others to remind him of their musical mystery tour.

(So, that's what she had bought in the museum's gift-shop!)

Chapter 5

Detective Books

It was night-time and Tali was fast asleep in his cosy bed in the roof of the library-van.   He was dreaming of scoring the winning goal at football for Scotland in the World Cup.

When he went up to collect the trophy, his medal seemed to be made from an oatcake and it broke when Ringo Starr pinned it to his shirt.

It was a weird dream!

Suddenly, Tali was awake!

He could hear a noise down in the library. Someone was moving about down there.

Tali jumped out of bed and quietly dreeped down into the van.

(Remember, he had to dreep because the book-stairs had returned to the book-shelves during the night.)

Whoever was down there must have heard Tali coming because he or she ran out of the door. It was too dark for Tali to see who had been there.

Tali switched on the light in the van and had a look around to see if anything was missing. He noticed a few gaps in the book-shelves. Some books had been stolen!

Next morning, Tali decided to become a detective. He would try to find out who had taken his books.

He spoke to the books on either side of the gaps and asked them which titles had been there the previous night. The books were happy to help and Tali soon had a list of the missing items.

On the list were:

- *The Fantastic Mr Fox*
- *The Fox's Socks*
- *That's Not My Fox*
- *The Fox who Came to Tea*
- *Goldilocks and the Three Foxes*

(Can you see a connection between all these books?)

Tali wondered if this was a clue to the identity of the thief. His nose began to twitch a little bit.

(Who do you think it could be?)

Tali thought that it might be a fox who would be interested in these stories. But, how could he find the thief?

Then he noticed a small piece of paper on the floor by the door of the van. He picked it up and saw that it was a bus ticket. Tali could see from the ticket that someone had come there by bus from Musselburgh the night before. The same night that the books were stolen!

"The thief might live in Musselburgh", thought Tali to himself, "I'll go there and see if I can find him". His nose twitched a bit more.

So, after breakfast, Tali and Esmerelda set off for Musselburgh. Esmerelda thought she was like the 'Mystery Machine' van in the Scooby-Doo programmes and she was looking forward to seeing the 'unmasking' of the baddie who had stolen the books.

When they arrived in Musselburgh, Tali used his clever nose to sniff out the books. The scent took him to a house which had the name "Mr N. Fox" on the nameplate beside the door.

"I bet the 'N.' stands for 'Naughty'", thought Tali as he rang the doorbell.

The fox looked out of the window and saw that it was Tali at the door.

The magic books also knew that Tali had come to rescue them and started to chat excitedly to one another.

"Good old Tali", said *The Fantastic Mr Fox.*

"He's come to save us", said *The Fox who Came to Tea.*

All of Tali's other stolen books joined in the chatter and the fox was worried that Tali might hear them.

"Oh no!" he cried, "What will I do? I'll need to hide the books … but first I'll need to stop them from talking".

When Tali's magic books talk, the pages open and close like little mouths.

Naughty Mr Naughty Fox took some ribbons and tied all of Tali's books tightly shut so that they could not speak. Then, he hid them on a high bookshelf beside his own books.

He put on a white wig and a pair of glasses to disguise himself as an old woman. Then he went to answer the door.

"Ah! Mr Tali Bookhound. It's good to see you. Come in", said the fox-granny.

Tali went into the fox's living-room and sat down on a chair.

"I've lost some very precious books from my library", said Tali, "I wonder if you've seen them?"

"No. I have not", said the fox-granny.

(Of course, the fox was lying; just like he had been when he said he had not seen Trevor's shoes in 'The Rabbit with Three Ears'.)

"Would you like a cup of tea?" he (or she) asked Tali.

"No thank you. I'm too busy. I must find my books", said Tali.

He did not really believe the stories he was hearing because the name-plate on the door had said 'Mister N Fox' not 'Mrs N Fox'.

His nose twitched a lot because he sensed that someone was trying to trick him.

All this time, Tali's books were trying to shout out to him:

"We're here, Tali"

... but it just sounded like,

"MMMM MMMM MM-MM"

... because the books were tied shut.

(You try saying "We're here Tali" with your lips held shut.)

Eventually, *'The Fox's Socks'* managed to wriggle out from between the books on either side of it and fell down from the shelf.

When it hit the floor, the ribbon came loose and it managed to shout:

"We're here, Tali"

... properly.

Tali picked up his brave book and started to search the fox's shelf for the others which had been taken from his library. When he found them all, he knew that the old lady fox was a baddie.

He 'unmasked' the fox by pulling off the wig and glasses.

"AHA! Got you!" said Tali.

"You know, Mr Fox, you don't need to steal books from my library. I come to Musselburgh every Tuesday and you can borrow them".

Tali made him a library card and the fox said 'sorry' and promised to be good in future. *(He says that a lot; doesn't he?)*

Tali went back to the library-van. *(Guess what he saw stuck to the end of his desk? ... That's right, a new magnet.)*

This magnet was in the shape of a magnifying-glass

... just like the ones that real detectives use!

Chapter 6

Cookery Books

Tali was exhausted after solving the *'Mystery of the Missing Books'* and so he decided to stay in Musselburgh. He parked Esmerelda near the little theatre and settled down for the night. As soon as his head hit the pillow, he was asleep … and dreaming …

Once again, it was a weird dream!

In his dream, he was on a bus. Lady Penelope from *Thunderbirds* was driving it! When he went upstairs, all the Tracy brothers were there in their *International Rescue* uniforms. They were sharing a big bag of Haribo Mix and they all started to shout at Brains because he took the 'fried egg' sweetie.

When Tali woke up, he felt better. He had a sausage-roll for his breakfast and then drove to the Botanic Gardens in Edinburgh. He parked Esmerelda outside the gate and waited for his customers to arrive.

First of all, came two children: a brother and sister called Tom and Rosie.

"Good morning", said Tali, "How can I help you today?"

"It's our Mummy's birthday soon and we'd like to cook dinner for her as a surprise", said Rosie.

"But we don't know what to cook", said Tom.

"And we don't know how to cook either", added his sister.

There was a flash in Tali's desk drawer. He opened it and took out a book called:

How to Cook

(That was lucky, wasn't it?)

"Try this", said Tali, "It should give you some ideas of what to make and it will tell you what to do. Just follow the instructions carefully."

Off they set with the cookery book, very excited about making dinner for their Mummy.

But ... a little while later they came back.

What a mess they were in; covered in flour and tomatoes with sticky mixture in their hair!

They told Tali that they had tried to make pizza and apple crumble but it hadn't worked.

"Please help", they pleaded.

"Hmmmm, let's see now", said Tali as he opened his desk drawer.

He took out a book called:

Home Cooking

By

Lorna Bookhound

... and placed it on the magic book-stand.

As soon Tali opened the book, something very strange started to happen.

"You'd better sit down and hold on tight", he told the children as he opened the book.

Rosie and Tom (who were still covered in tomatoes and flour and sticky mixture) held each other's hand as they stared in amazement at the spinning books.

Some books leapt off the shelves and flew around as if they were caught up in whirlwind tornado.

The van's door closed itself and the other books on the shelves started to go round and round.

When they stopped spinning and the door opened, Esmerelda was sitting in the front garden of a little house. There was a sign on the gate saying:

Thistledown Cottage

"This is my granny's house", said Tali, "She's a great cook and I'm sure she'll be happy to show you what to do. Watch and listen carefully".

The children followed the little, old lady into the kitchen of her cottage, which was sparkling clean.

Tali's Granny, Lorna Bookhound showed Rosie and Tom how to cook her favourite things.

These were:

- Tattie soup
  - Tatties are what she calls potatoes
- Scones
  - She made cheese scones and fruit scones
- Skirlie
  - This is made with oatmeal and onions and you have it with mince or chicken and gravy

The children listened as hard as they could but there was a lot to remember. They got to taste all of the delicious things Granny Lorna made and it was all yummy ... but soon it was time to go home.

They said "Goodbye" and got back into the library-van. Tali closed the cookery book on the magic stand and the books on the shelves started to spin the other way. Soon they were all back in Edinburgh.

As they left the van, Rosie said, "Thanks Tali. It's Mummy's birthday tomorrow. We'll let you know how we get on with cooking her dinner." ... and they did!

The next time Tali and Esmerelda were at the Botanics in Edinburgh, the two children came back to the library.

They brought a magnet in the shape of a birthday cake for Tali's desk.

"How did you get on with the birthday dinner?" asked Tali.

"Well, we remembered most of the things your Granny cooked", said Tom.

(Do you remember what they had learned to make?)

- *Cheese scones and fruit scones*
- *Mince or chicken and gravy with skirlie*
- *Tattie soup*

"But we got a bit jumbled up", said Rosie.

"We made:

- Chicken with cheese and fruit
- Scones with gravy
- Mince soup
- Tatties and skirlie

"They didn't look or taste like the yummy things your Granny made for us", said Tom.

"But, Mummy did try to eat everything we made and she said that the tatties and skirlie were her favourite", said Rosie.

"Oh well, at least you tried and I'm sure your Mummy was pleased", said Tali.

What he REALLY thought was:

"Scones with Gravy? … Mince Soup? … YUK!"

Chapter 7

Do-It-Yourself Books

Tali woke up from a lovely sleep. He had been dreaming again but this time it was not his usual 'weird' type of dream, it was quite nice.

He dreamt he was eating a big, white marshmallow. It was really huge! Tali lay back in his bed thinking about how delicious it had been.

Then he opened his eyes and got a big surprise.

There was a massive hole in his pillow!

He had taken a bite out of it while he was dreaming about the marshmallow. Poor old Tali; his mouth was very dry from chewing his pillow so he had some extra juicy blueberries with his porridge that morning.

Even after his breakfast, he still had little feathers sticking to his whiskers!

He drove Esmerelda to Silverknowes and parked near the beach. He did not have to wait long for his first customer of the day.

Along came a man called Angus who said that he had just joined the local sailing club and needed a boat.

"But this is a library, not a boatyard", said Tali.

"Yes, I know that", said Angus, "I don't want to <u>buy</u> a boat, I'd like to <u>make</u> one myself. Do you have any Do-It-Yourself books?"

"Yes, I have the very thing for you", said Tali as the drawer in his desk flashed, "Here, have a look at this".

Tali handed over a big, thick book with lots of pages.

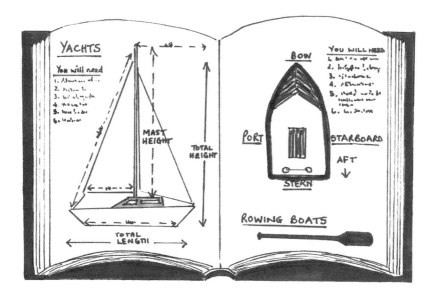

It was full of diagrams showing how to build a boat. It was just like the instructions you get with Lego Star Wars kits, but much, much more complicated.

"Great, thanks!" said Angus, "but I don't have any tools. Do you know anyone who has hammers and saws and drills and nails?"

"In fact, I do know the very person", replied Tali. He took out his phone and used the 'Supercats' app to make a non-emergency request for help.

(In case you don't remember, that's the amber button on the app.)

Soon, Gerard Supercat came flying in. Now, Gerard had not been a real Supercat for very long and was still not used to flying as he had only had his cape for a few months.

He tried to land beside the library-van but crashed into the roof and landed on Tali's bed. He had to dreep down to meet Tali and Angus.

"Why is there a big hole in your pillow?" he asked Tali.

"Never mind that!" said Tali, with his face going red, "Angus here wants you to help him to build this boat".

Tali handed the instruction book to Gerard, pointing at the boat which Angus had chosen. But he forgot how clumsy Gerard was.

Gerard dropped the book and all the pages fell out onto the floor of the van.

"Ooopsee!" he said and started to pick them up again.

"OK, you two get on with building the boat and I'll come and see how you're getting on when I've finished lending books", said Tali.

Gerard and Angus started work, using all the Supercat's tools. It took them ages and they made sure they followed the instructions precisely.

When Tali came along to see how they were getting on he saw something very strange. Instead of building a long, flat boat, they had built a tall, thin tower.

Unfortunately, when Gerard had picked up all the pages of the book, he had put them back in the wrong way round.

"Oh No!" cried Angus.

"Never mind", said Gerard, "instead of a boat's propeller, we can add a booster and turn it into a rocket!"

At least he did not suggest using a hairdryer like the last time he tried to make a booster rocket for his scooter. The hairdryer was no use at all because it had to be plugged into the wall. (*Do you remember?*)

Angus was not very pleased. "But, I wanted a boat", he said, although he agreed to try out the rocket anyway.

(*I think Angus is just about as crazy as Gerard, don't you?*)

So, they fitted a booster to the boat-rocket and prepared for blast-off.

Angus jumped into the driving seat and Gerard leapt in beside him.

"Come on, Tali!" they shouted, "There's plenty of room".

"No, thanks", he replied, remembering Gerard's past experiences of technical disasters.

5-4-3-2-1

WE-HAVE-LIFT-OFF!

The rocket shot up into the air over the River Forth towards Fife.

"WEE-HEE", shouted Gerard while Angus tried to control the boat-rocket.

Suddenly, it veered to the left and started heading for the huge, red, metal Forth Bridge. It shot under the span which holds the railway line. People on a train on the bridge were shocked to see a rocket zoom under them.

Next, the boat-rocket rose up into the air and just missed the tall towers of the Forth Road Bridge.

Then it pointed downwards again and passed under the new, 3rd bridge which had just been built. The boat-rocket splashed into the water under the bridge.

"WOO-HOO", cried Gerard, "Now we're in a submarine".

Angus was still desperately trying to steer the boat-rocket-submarine towards dry land. He wanted to get off.

It eventually shot out of the water and onto the beach at Silverknowes, near where Tali stood watching with his mouth wide open in shock.

The two adventurers climbed out onto the sand. Gerard's eyes were wide with excitement, while Angus was trying not to cry.

"Let's do it again!" shouted Gerard.

"No, let's not!" said Angus, "I've decided Do-It-Yourself boats are not a good idea. I'm going to buy myself a new boat; one which just stays on the surface of the water."

Tali gave him a magazine which showed pictures of lots of boats for sale.

They decided to leave the boat-rocket-submarine on the beach and turn it into a boat-rocket-submarine-ice-cream-shop.

Gerard Supercat flew home and Tali shut the library for the night.

He noticed a new magnet on the side of his desk.

It was like a boat but it was pointing up in the air like a rocket.

Tali turned it so it was the right way round but …

… as soon as he looked away …

… the magnet turned itself round to look like a rocket again!

As he climbed up the book-stairs at bedtime, Tali remembered the hole in his pillow.

"I'll buy a new pillow tomorrow", he said and turned the holey pillow over.

"I just hope I don't dream about marshmallows again tonight", he thought sleepily as he snuggled down in his cosy bed.

Chapter 8

History Books

Tali did have a dream that night, but it was not about marshmallows. It was about his favourite banana cake which his granny bakes for him whenever he visits her.

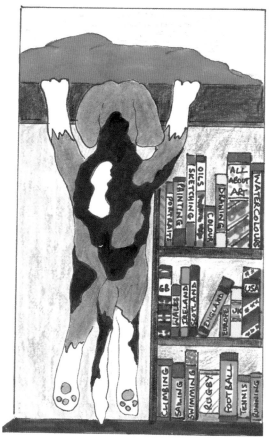

"I must go and see my Granny soon", he thought as he dreeped down into the library the next morning.

He drove the library-van to Linlithgow, stopping to buy some cereal in a café for his breakfast.

Soon after he opened the door of the van, a little boy called Guy came in. He did not look very happy.

"What's wrong?" asked Tali.

"My mum says I've to get out of the house. She says I spend too much time playing games on the computer. She says <u>she</u> always played outside when <u>she</u> was young. But that was in the olden-days. It's really BORING outside", he complained.

Tali said it wasn't really 'the olden days' when his mum was young.

"That would be only about 20 or 30 years ago. Imagine living 5,000 years ago", he said.

"5,000 years ago!" cried Guy, "Nobody was alive then, surely".

"Oh, yes", said Tali, "Have a look in the 'HISTORY' section over there and see what takes your fancy".

"Do I have to?" Guy moaned.

"Go on, have a look and see what happens", urged Tali.

Guy looked at all the books on the shelves and saw that one was sticking out a little bit. It was called:

Ancient Orkney

The book seemed to want him to pick it but he just pushed it back beside the other books on the shelf.

He then saw another book called:

The History of Computer Games

"That's more like it", he said and took that book over to Tali's desk.

When Guy put the book on the desk, Tali said, "Good choice, my friend". He had a strange smile on his face.

When Guy looked down, the book had changed. It was now called:

Ancient Orkney

Somehow, the books had swapped themselves over. How could this have happened? He had held the book in his hands all the way from the shelf to the desk.

(It must be magic!)

Tali just smiled.

He put the book on the special stand on his desk and warned Guy to sit down as he opened it.

The book-shelves started doing their spinny thing and Guy grabbed onto the desk as he was feeling a bit dizzy.

Soon the spinning stopped and Tali opened the door of the van.

"Welcome to Skara Brae … 5,000 years ago", said Tali as he led the way outside.

The library-van was parked in a little hollow in the ground, surrounded by trees. Camper-vans, like Esmerelda, had not been invented this long ago and Tali did not want anyone to see her.

As they walked out of the woods, they could see a village made up of small, round houses. The walls were made from piles of stones and the roofs seemed to be covered over with grass.

As they approached the village, they saw a young boy of about Guy's age coming out of one of the houses. He had to bend down very low to get out of the door.

"Hello there", he said when he saw Guy and Tali, "My name's Magnus. Would you like to help me with my chores?"

Tali and Guy introduced themselves to Magnus and said they would help. Guy was not too keen at first, saying he'd rather play a game. After Tali explained that there was no electricity, never mind any computers, Guy decided that he'd lend a hand.

First, they went to collect vegetables to make soup for Magnus's lunch. It was useful that Tali was a hound-dog as he chased away a few rabbits who were munching Magnus's carrots. Guy had never seen how vegetables grow and he was amazed at how delicious they all looked. Magnus showed him how to pop open pea-pods and eat the yummy peas raw.

Next, they went down to the beach to collect wood to make a fire to cook the vegetables. There were no microwave ovens in Skara Brae.

The two boys had fun throwing small pebbles into the sea while Tali splashed about in the waves.

When it was getting dark and it was time for Tali and Guy to go home, Magnus produced a beautiful pebble from his pocket and gave it to Guy.

"I found this on the beach years ago and I've been polishing it every night before I go to sleep. I'd like you to have it to remind you of your visit to Orkney", he said.

"Thanks a lot. I'll try to remember to polish it every night too", said Guy.

He searched in his own pockets to see if there was anything he could give to Magnus in return. All he could find was a piece of bright orange Lego and a Super-Zing. He gave them both to Magnus and said that he'd had a lovely day.

Magnus had never seen plastic things before *(it had not been invented yet)* so he was amazed. He said he'd keep them safe and treasure them forever.

Tali and Guy got back into the library-van and closed the door. Tali shut the book on the stand and the book-shelves spun backwards bringing the van back to Linlithgow in modern times.

A new magnet with a map of Orkney had appeared on the side of his desk and Tali and Guy tried to find Magnus's beach on it. They had to use a magnifying glass to because the map was so small.

Tali decided to spend the night in Linlithgow as he was tired from running after rabbits in Orkney. He said good-night to Guy and crept up to his bed.

When Guy got home, his mum was pleased to hear that he'd had a good day 'outside'. He did not tell her that they'd been to Orkney 5,000 years ago. She would not have believed him if he had.

Guy put the polished pebble beside his computer to remind him of Magnus. It also reminded him to go outside to play sometimes.

Chapter 9

Gardening Books

The very next morning after the trip to Orkney, Tali was fast asleep in his cosy bed up in the roof of the library-van. He was having a lovely dream.

In his dream, he was in his Granny's living-room. She was doing her usual trick of knitting and reading a magazine and watching the TV; all at the same time. He asked her what she would like for her birthday and she thought carefully then said:

'BANG BANG BANG'

"What!?" asked Tali.

'BANG BANG BANG BANG'

... repeated Granny.

(Huh??)

Suddenly, Tali woke up and realised that the banging noise was not coming from his Granny in the dream, but from the door down in the van.

Tali pulled on his dressing-gown and dreeped down into the library.

When he opened the door, there stood Guy, the boy from the day before.

When Guy saw that Tali was still wearing his dressing-gown, he realised that he must have woken up the bookhound from his sleep.

"Oh, sorry to wake you, Mr Bookhound, but I wanted to make sure I got a book before you drove off to your next town".

"Well, first of all, call me Tali. Now, what kind of book do you need so urgently that it can't wait until I come back next week?" said Tali, yawning.

"I'd like a book which shows me how to grow carrots and peas. I'd love to have a vegetable garden like Magnus had in Skara Brae", said Guy, excitedly. "My mum says I can have a small bit of our garden at home to grow things".

Tali thought that Guy seemed very different from the bored and unhappy boy who had come to the library-van the day before.

Different in a good way, though!

"Let's see what Esmerelda can find for you", said Tali, pleased that Guy was interested in something other than computer games.

The very happy boy started browsing the book-shelves in the 'GARDENING' section of the library while Tali went to get dressed and ready for the day …

… Tali had not even brushed his teeth yet.

Guy found lots of books on different types of gardening:

- Landscape Gardening
    - For big parks and gardens in castles
- Bonsai
    - A Japanese type of garden where they grow tiny trees
- Flower Growing and Arranging
    - This book said to make sure to put flowers in the vase with the coloured bits pointing upwards, not upside down! *(Very good advice)*
- Market Gardening
    - Guy had been to Craigie's Farm which is quite near his house. They grow lots of vegetables there, but it's huge!

"These all seem like very useful books for certain things, but not exactly what I need", sighed Guy when Tali came back down *(with his hair nicely brushed)*.

Tali twitched his nose and the top drawer in his desk flashed.

"What have we here?" he said, handing Guy the book he found in his drawer.

Vegetable Growing for Beginners

... "the very thing. Look, the book even comes with a selection of seeds ready for you to plant".

Guy was delighted!

"Thanks, Mr Bookhound ... I mean Tali", he said and sped off home with the book under his arm.

Guy's mum was so pleased that he was keen to do things outdoors that she had bought him a small fork and spade. He used these to turn over all the soil in his special vegetable patch.

Guy kept the book beside him and it told him what to do. Whenever he did something wrong, the book would say, "No, not there; over there" or "those potatoes are too close together" or "plant those peas a bit deeper in the ground".

There were hundreds of things to remember!

But after a few weeks, things started to grow!

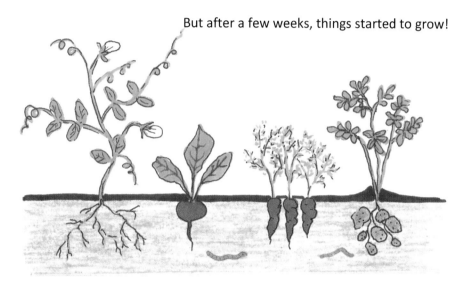

Peas and potatoes and carrots started to sprout from the ground. Soon, Guy could recognise the different vegetables by just looking at their leaves.

With the book's help, Guy spent the summer getting everything right:

- tying up pea plants
- digging out weeds
- watering the plants
- digging out weeds
- thinning out carrots
- digging out weeds

There were ***lots*** of weeds!

Along with the vegetable seeds which came with the book, there was a packet of sunflower-seeds. Guy had planted these too and he was pleased to see them growing.

He had also planted four Lego bricks hoping they would grow into full Lego Star Wars kits but, sadly, that did not work!

(Good try, Guy!)

As summer wore on, just before it was time to go back to school after the holidays, his little patch was bursting with vegetables.

Guy thought it would be nice to thank Tali for his help. He decided to make a big pot of soup and take it to the library-van.

He used peas, carrots, onions, chicken, potatoes, leeks and turnips; almost everything came from his vegetable plot.

(Can you guess which item he did NOT grow himself?

That's right, he bought the chicken from his local supermarket.)

Tali was very pleased with the soup and said it was yummy.

Guy gave Tali a new magnet in the shape of a carrot.

He also gave him another magnet like a piece of Lego and told him that, sadly, Lego does not grow in gardens.

(This was something which Tali already knew).

On the last day of the school holidays, Guy picked a big bunch of the sunflowers from his garden and gave them to his mum.

He was very proud to have produced his very own flowers.

"Thanks Mum", he said, "Gardening is much better fun than playing computer games".

Guy's mum said that she was proud of him and gave him a big squeezy hug.

Chapter 10

Joke Books

One day, a girl called Sandie came into the library-van. Her teacher at school had asked everyone to perform something in front of the class the next day.

They could each choose from:

- Dancing
- Singing
- Playing a musical instrument
- Performing magic tricks
- Telling jokes

Sandie was not sure what she wanted to do so she wandered about in front of all the book-shelves looking for ideas. As she did so, one book slid out from the others and stuck out in front of her. It was on the bottom shelf so she did not see it.

She tripped over the sticking-out book and fell onto the floor.

"Hey! What's going on?" she shouted with surprise.

Then she saw the name of the book which was lying on the floor. It was called:

The Trickster's Book of Tricky Tricks

"That might be just what I'm looking for", thought Sandie as she picked it up.

On the front cover was a picture of a fireman standing in front of his fire-engine holding a hose. One of the wheels of the engine looked like a big button and there were some words saying:

'Press me to hear the fire-engine's siren'

Sandie pressed the button but, instead of hearing the siren, some water came scooshing out of the hose and squirted right in her face. She was soaked.

A few of the other books on the shelves around her started to giggle.

"Not funny!" she said, huffily.

Next, Sandie opened the book and a big boxing-glove sprang out and punched her on the nose.

The other books started to laugh and she had to give them a hard stare to make them stop.

(Can you do a hard stare?)

Sandie decided that the book was too tricky for her and she tried to put it back on the shelf. Suddenly, all of the other 'tricky' books shuffled along the shelf and closed the gap where it had been.

There was no room for it on the shelf anymore.

Just then, Tali appeared from the roof of the library-van.

"Good morning, Sandie", he said, "I see the trick books have been up to their usual tricks".

"Yes", replied Sandie, "I'm looking for a book with a lot of jokes or tricks in it; not one that plays tricks on me!"

"I think I've got the very thing for you", smiled Tali, as the drawer in his desk flashed.

He took out a book called:

The World's Greatest Jokes and Tricks

"Try this one", said Tali, "You will <u>definitely</u> get a laugh out of it".

Sandie did not really know what he meant by that but then Tali twitched his nose and the book opened at the 'JOKE' section.

There, Sandie found a button which said:

'Press me for a laugh'

She was a bit scared to press it, remembering that she had been soaked by the trick book.

She stood to the side and pressed the button with her arm stretched out.

Suddenly, the book let out a loud laughing noise.

"That's so you can practise telling jokes at home. The book will laugh at them for you", explained Tali.

Sandie thanked him and set off with the book.

That night, she studied very hard and tried to remember all the jokes and how to do the tricks.

In the 'TRICK' section of the book, she found two which she really liked:

Trick Number 1

In this trick, she appeared to pull her thumb apart into two pieces.

Trick Number 2

In this trick, a cup contained one large black dice which changed into several small white dice when she shook it.

Sandie practiced both tricks and got quite good at them.

It really looked like she had pulled her thumb apart!

In the 'JOKE' section, she chose two of her favourites:

Joke Number 1

Knock Knock

Who's there?

The interrupting cow

The interrupt...   MOOOO!

Joke Number 2

What's orange and sounds like a parrot?

I don't know

A carrot

Sandie thought that the tricks would be too hard for all of her class to see from a distance so she decided to tell the two jokes instead. She just hoped that she could remember what to say.

She practised all evening using the book's laughter button to get used to people laughing at her jokes.

The next morning, Sandie was very nervous about standing up in front of her class. When she arrived at school, she was pleased to see Tali's library-van parked in the playground.

Other boys and girls took turns in performing their songs and dances. No-one else seemed to have chosen to tell jokes, which pleased Sandie. It would be awful if someone else told her jokes before she did!

Tali stood at the back of the class and clapped after each performance.

When it came to her turn, she was even more nervous. She walked out to the front and stood beside the teacher's desk, but then ….

OH NO!

She could not remember her jokes. She just stood there, saying nothing.

Then Tali saved the day! He pretended to knock on the wall of the classroom and silently mouthed the word 'MOOOO!' for Sandie to see. This reminded Sandie of her first joke and she told it well. The whole class laughed when she interrupted the teacher.

Next, Tali held up two pictures; one of a parrot and one of a carrot. Again, this was enough to remind Sandie of her second joke. She told it well and the whole class laughed again.

Sandie thanked Tali for his help and said that she did not feel so nervous now that her first performance was over.

She said that she would like to do it again … some day.

Sandie gave Tali a magnet in the shape of a cow saying "MOOOO".

She noticed that he already had a carrot magnet. *(Do you remember who gave it to him?)*

Chapter 11

Art Books

Esmerelda was parked in Bonnyrigg and Tali was ready for the day.

He'd had a great sleep the night before with no weird dreams. He'd also eaten a big bowl of porridge with banana for his breakfast and the sun was shining.

A girl called Evie came into the library-van.

"Good morning, Tali. What do you know about painting?" she asked.

"Well, I know you use one type of paint on the walls and ceiling and a different type of paint on the doors when you are painting a house. And you don't put any paint on the glass in the windows", he replied.

"No, not that kind of painting!" she shouted, "Painting pictures!"

Tali said that he knew a little bit about Art and asked Evie what she wanted to know.

"I've always been interested in drawing", she said.

"First, I did colouring in. That's where you get a picture which just has the outlines drawn and you have to use coloured pens or pencils to fill in all the spaces. You have to be careful not to go over the lines. I like it because you can choose any colours you like", Evie told him.

"Yes, I believe it's very popular with grown-ups too these days", replied Tali.

"Next, I moved on to sketching" Evie told Tali. "I asked my mum for some blank paper and made up my own drawings. It's a bit more difficult but I like it. It means that I can create any pictures I want."

"Here's one I did of 'King Cactus' with his crown", said Evie, proudly.

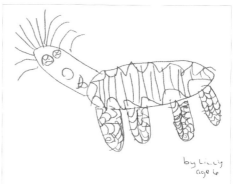

by Lilly age 6

"The other was drawn by my sister, Lilly, who is 6", she added.

"They are both very good", said Tali, "but how can I help you today?"

"I'd like to see pictures of paintings that other people have done; to give me ideas about how I should paint. Do you have any books like that in the library-van?" she asked.

"Have a look in the 'ART' section and see if there is anything you like", Tali suggested.

Evie found lots of different books about famous artists and their paintings.

Each artist seemed to have their own style:

- Salvador Dali had painted watches melting off of tables and elephants on long spindly legs, like stilts
- John Constable was good at painting the countryside with lots of rivers and ponds
- Vincent Van Gogh seemed to like painting with dark blues and dusky yellow shades
- Pablo Picasso's paintings were just weird *(according to Evie)*

Her favourite artist was Edgar Degas who seemed to like to paint ballet dancers. Evie took his book from the shelf and took it over to Tali's desk.

"Look at all these beautiful dresses", she sighed, "I wish I could see some of his real paintings!"

"But, you can!" said Tali with a smile as he placed the Degas book in his special book-stand.

The van door closed and the book-shelves started spinning around. Evie grabbed her sketch-book and held on to it tightly. She did not want to be without it.

When the spinning stopped and the van door opened, they were outside the Scottish Portrait Gallery in Edinburgh.

They went inside and asked the man at the reception desk if they had any paintings by Hilaire-Germain-Edgar Degas.

(Evie found his full name in the book from the library. It's very long, isn't it? His friends just call him 'Edgar'.)

The man typed a few things into his computer.

"Well, the gallery does have some pieces by Degas but they are mostly sculptures. We do have one painting but it's not on display at present. It's in our storage cupboard" he said.

"What good is that?" thought Evie.

"Why would you have a beautiful painting and keep it in a cupboard?" she asked.

"That's just stupid!" she added.

The man said he didn't know why they kept so many pictures in a cupboard and Evie thought that he didn't care either.

Tali suggested that they should have a look at some other paintings while they were there. He could see she was very disappointed.

"We could have a look at the Degas ballet sculptures too", he added, trying to cheer her up.

The gallery did have some beautiful sculptures of ballet dancers. Evie's favourite sculpture was of a lady dancer with a gold top and a white tutu.

Evie was delighted when she saw that the gallery did have a portrait of the *Supercats*, Misha and Gerard. She took out a pencil and started to sketch it on her pad.

In the portrait on the wall, Misha smiled happily and Gerard turned his head to show off what he thought was the handsomest side of his face.

As Evie worked on her drawing, the Gerard in the portrait kept peering over; trying to see what she was doing.

Evie was very pleased with her sketch and so she went into the gallery shop and bought a magnet with the picture of the *Supercats* on it.

When they got back to the library-van, Tali could see that Evie was still disappointed at not having seen any paintings by Degas.

"Time for action", he thought.

Tali opened the book at a different page (one with lots of Degas ballerinas on it) and the van set off on its travels again.

When the door opened, they found themselves outside the art gallery in London where Martha and Mary had been locked in overnight.

(Do you remember that story? A policeman mistakenly thought that they were robbers and put them in jail!)

This gallery had one Degas painting of ballet dancers and it was NOT in a cupboard. Evie was delighted to see it and started to copy it into her sketch-book.

She was even more delighted when Tali took her to a real ballet show that afternoon. She sat in the balcony and made lots of drawings of the dancers in their frilly dresses.

It was quite tricky to draw the dancers because they kept moving about.

"I wish they would keep still so I can draw them", said Evie.

Tali decided to help her out. He twitched his magic nose and something amazing happened.

The music stopped! It was completely silent and the dancers all froze and stood still!

It was as if they were playing 'Musical Statues'.

One of the lady dancers was balancing on one leg. Another man was holding a dancer up in the air above his head.

Evie finished her drawing as quickly as she could because she did not want the dancers to hurt themselves.

When she was finished drawing, Tali twitched his nose for a second time and the music and dancing started up again.

No-one else seemed to notice that it had even stopped!

Soon, it was time to go home and so Tali and Evie went back into the library-van.

When they arrived back in Bonnyrigg, Evie thanked Tali for all his kindness.

She said she had loved all the pictures in the galleries and the dancers at the ballet.

"They have given me lots of ideas about what I should paint", she added.

Evie gave Tali the Supercat magnet which she had bought in the Scottish Portrait Gallery's gift shop.

She used the magnet to stick one of her own drawings of the ballet dancers to the side of Tali's desk.

Chapter 12

Outdoor Activity Books

One morning, Tali was waking up from a long, cosy sleep. He was still snuggled up under his quilt, hugging his pillow.

(He had bought a new one after he chewed a hole in the old one!)

He did not really want to be awake yet and so he just opened one eye to see what the rest of the world was doing …

… and there was a face staring right into his!

"AAAARRRRGGGGHHHHH", he shouted as he sat straight up in his bed.

"Sorry Tali. I didn't mean to give you a fright", said the face.

"What are you doing in my bedroom?" he demanded.

"I'm not <u>in</u> your bedroom", said the face, "I'm outside on the roof of your van".

"Well, get down IMMEDIATELY", said Tali, fully awake now.

Tali dreeped down into the library and opened the door of the van. A girl was waiting outside. It was her face that Tali had seen at his bedroom window.

"Sorry again, Tali", she said, "My name is Lilly".

"How did you get onto the roof of the library-van?" Tali asked her.

"Well, I couldn't sleep and I was bored so I decided to make a rope-swing. I put a long rope over a high branch of one of the trees in the woods beside your van. I was swinging backwards and forwards; going higher and higher", explained Lilly.

"It was very exciting!" she squealed.

"But I swung so high that I could not hold on. My hands slipped and I went flying off and landed on the roof of the library-van".

"That sounds a bit dangerous", said Tali.

"Not really", said Lilly, "I do things like that all the time. I love having adventures. My mum says I'm a real daredevil".

"Well, maybe we should find some less daring adventures for you to try out. Go and have a look in the library".

Lilly had a look in the 'OUTDOOR ACTIVITIES' section and saw a book called:

Forest-Craft – Living in the Woods

"That looks interesting", she thought and flicked through the book. She saw a section on how to build a shelter from branches and twigs and decided she would have a go at it.

"I'm going to sleep in the woods!" she told Tali.

"Splendid idea! Here, you'll probably need this", he replied and handed Lilly an empty jam jar.

"What's that for?" she asked.

"I'm sure you can find a use for it", he replied with a knowing smile.

(What do you think it might be used for?)

Lilly chose a good spot under a tall tree and laid long branches up against the tree-trunk. Then she wove twigs between the branches to make a kind of wall. Finally she spread leaves over the twigs to make a cosy nest for herself.

Inside, she used piles of leaves to make a soft bed to lie on.

After her den was complete, Lilly picked some wild raspberries and brambles for her supper (the book told her which ones were safe to eat). Then she decided that it was time to go to bed. As she snuggled up in her soft leaf-bed, she got a big surprise.

Something was jagging into her bottom.

Suddenly a little head popped out of the leaves.

It was a hedgehog!

She had scooped it up by mistake when she was collecting the leaves. She gave it some of her raspberries to say 'sorry' for stealing its bed. The hedgehog thought that the berries were yummy and stuffed lots into its mouth.

It was starting to get dark in the woods and Lilly was having trouble reading her book. There were no bedside lamps there in the woods. Then she saw tiny specks of light flying around between the trees.

They were fireflies!

Fireflies are a type of flying beetle. Their bodies glow with light in the dark.

Lilly asked the fireflies if they would mind lending her their light to help her to read her book. They said, "Sure, no problem!" and they flew into the empty jam jar which Tali had given her.

Their light shone through the glass just like a torch and Lilly could see well enough to read her book.

(So, that's why Tali gave her the empty jam jar. Clever Tali!)

After a while, Lilly fell asleep beside the hedgehog who was snoring gently, full of raspberries. The fireflies also settled down to sleep and their light went dim, just like the lamp Lilly had in her bedroom at home.

Suddenly, Lilly was wakened by a loud:

"WOOOO WOOOO"

It sounded like a ghost and she was a bit scared. She tried to wake the hedgehog but he was fast asleep, dreaming of raspberries.

The firefly-torch became bright again and Lilly looked in her forest-craft book to find out what was making the noise.

(Can you guess what it was?)

It was an owl. Lilly checked her book and it told her that most owls sleep during the day and are awake at night. She was not scared of owls.

Lilly was soon fast asleep again … but not for long.

Soon the sunshine was streaming in through the twigs of her den. She opened the jar and let the fireflies out, saying "Thanks for your help" as the beetles flew back into the woods.

Lilly ran over to Tali's van and knocked on the door. She did not realise how early it was.

Tali opened the door of the van and was very surprised to see Lilly.

"What are you doing here at this time? It's only 5 o'clock in the morning", muttered a very sleepy Tali.

"Oops, Sorry Tali. I don't have any curtains in my tree-shelter so the sun came shining in as soon as it was daytime" she explained.

"Anyway life's too exciting to spend time being asleep. I'm a daredevil. I want more adventures", she cried.

Tali let her come into the library-van while he went back up to his bed. It was so early that the books had not even put themselves back on the shelves yet.

As he climbed back up the book-staircase, Tali saw that a new magnet had appeared on his desk. It was a jam-jar full of fireflies. He noticed that the new magnet had a button which said 'PRESS ME'.

When Tali pressed the button, each firefly started to flash on and off with tiny sparks of light.

Although Tali was very sleepy, Lilly was wide awake and keen to have more fun.

Luckily, the library-van had a large 'ADVENTURE' section and Lilly went straight there.

"What can I do next?" she asked herself.

We'll hear what other adventures she gets up to next time.

Chapter 13

Adventure Books

Lilly was still in the 'ADVENTURE' section of the library while Tali finally dreeped down from his bed.

She soon found the book she was looking for, with a little help from the book itself. She started to run her hand along the books to help her choose the one she wanted. Every time she moved her hand along the shelf, this book moved along too. She eventually decided that this must be the book for her and she took it from the shelf.

It was called:

Adventure Stories for Young Daredevils

It had pictures of dragons and pirates and fairgrounds and circuses on the cover so Lilly thought it was perfect.

She took the book over to Tali's desk.

As Tali opened the book and placed it on the special stand on his desk, he quickly grabbed an apple from his fruit-bowl.

"It's turning out to be quite an exciting day!" he thought, "and I haven't even had my breakfast yet".

When the books stopped spinning and the van's door opened, they found themselves in a big park. A sign on the fence said **'RUSKIN PARK'**.

"There are lots of exciting things to do here", Tali told Lilly, "Let's start with the trapeze, since you like swinging on ropes".

High above them were two wooden bars hanging from long ropes. Tali explained that the idea was to hold on to the bar and swing back and forward. Another person would swing on the other bar. The two people would swing far apart, then close together. When they came together, one person would let go of their bar, fly through the air and be caught by the other person.

"YIPPEE, I can't wait to try that!" said Lilly, excitedly, but then she looked a bit worried. "What happens if you miss me and I fall?" she asked.

"Don't worry. There's a big safety-net above the ground to catch you", said Tali.

So Tali went up and held on to one trapeze and Lilly began swinging from the other one. Each time they swung close together, Tali shouted instructions to Lilly. Then Tali turned around so that he was holding on to the bar with his legs. It was tucked in tightly behind his knees. This meant his hands were free to catch Lilly.

Lilly made an extra-strong swing and decided that the next time she swung close to Tali, she would let go and fly over to him.

But ...

As she swung forward, she looked over to the other trapeze. Tali was not there! Instead, there was a pirate swinging by his knees.

The pirate had shoved Tali off and he was lying on the safety-net below.

The pirate had a shiny metal hook in place of one of his hands and he tried to grab Lilly with it.

Tali shouted "Jump, Lilly!" and she let go of the trapeze. She landed in the safety-net beside Tali.

The two adventurers climbed down from the net and ran down the hill towards the paddling pond.

This pool of water was not very deep; not even up to Lilly's knees. Tali and Lilly were very hot from running away from the pirate so they soaked their feet in the lovely, cold water.

Suddenly, the water started to make big waves and out of one of these waves appeared a huge pirate ship! The pirate was standing on the deck and he leaned over the side and grabbed the belt of Lilly's shorts with his hook. He pulled her up onto the deck of beside him.

Tali was splashing about in the pond trying to get up onto the ship but it was too high.

He heard Lilly shouting for help and looked up.

She was standing on the end of a long piece of wood which was sticking out over the side of the ship. The pirate was making her 'walk the plank' by pointing a sharp sword at her bottom.

One more step and Lilly would tumble off the end of the plank and into the water.

Just as she was about to fall, the sky went very dark as if the sun had gone behind a big, black cloud.

Everyone looked up *(even the pirate)* and saw a massive green dragon flying over the pond.

The dragon had huge claws and fire coming out of its mouth.

It swooped down and caught Lilly in its claws just before she hit the water.

The dragon carried Lilly over to Tali who was standing on the grass beside the paddling pond.

"There you are, Tali", said the dragon.

"Oh, thanks Debbie", said Tali and introduced Lilly to his friend.

"Debbie's fiery breath is very useful when I can't get my barbecue to light", he told Lilly as he winked at the Debbie the Dragon.

"That reminds me", said Debbie, "We're having lava for our tea tonight and I told my mum and dad I'd get some from a volcano on my way home from school. I'd better be off now. Nice to meet you, Lilly".

Debbie spread her wings and flew over the hill and far away.

Just then, the pirate and a few of his pals came running down the same hill waving swords and knives and calling the adventures terrible names.

(What names do you think they called Tali and Lilly?)

Tali and Lilly sped off to another area of the park where there was a fairground. There were lots of different things to ride on. People were shouting and screaming with delight as they sped round and round.

There were also gentle rides with cars and boats for young children.

Lilly was fascinated by all the bright lights and the loud noises. Then she remembered that the pirates were chasing them.

"They're coming, Tali! Where can we hide?" she shouted.

Then Tali saw a carousel. This is a big machine with lots of model animals attached to long poles. Children sit on the animals and hold on to the poles as the carousel goes round and round. This carousel played loud music and the animals moved up and down on the poles as it turned.

Tali jumped onto the carousel and leaned against one of the empty poles which held the roof up. He told Lilly to sit on his back and hold on to the pole. When the carousel started moving, Tali slid up and down the pole at the same time as all the other animals. He and Lilly just looked like part of the ride.

The pirates looked everywhere for the two adventurers but they could not find them. They finally got fed up and went back to their ship.

When the carousel stopped, Tali and Lilly got off and made their way back to the library-van.

They were exhausted.

"Well, I think that's enough adventures for one day", said Tali and Lilly agreed.

Lilly found a magnet in the pocket of her shorts and give it to Tali.

It was in the shape of a carousel.

If you looked really closely, you could see that one of the animals on it was a green dragon.

(What do you think the dragon on the carousel magnet was called?)

Chapter 14

Puzzle Books

One good thing about a mobile library is that it can travel about the country. You already know that Tali drives to lots of different towns in Esmerelda; but he can also visit people's houses.

If someone is ill or cannot walk, Tali can visit them at home to let them change their library books.

One day, twin brothers, Joe and Emmet, did not want to go to school so they pretended to be sick. Their Mummy contacted the school to tell them that the boys were ill and then she called Tali and asked if he could visit the boys because they were stuck at home.

Tali parked the van in their driveway and the boys came out in their pyjamas, slippers and dressing-gowns (DGs). They had to remember to walk slowly when their Mummy was looking so she would think that they really were ill.

Tali said that it was good to keep active when you are ill but the boys just said that they were too tired and winked at each other.

"Oh, we can't do anything hard like running or jumping", said Joe, weakly.

"Yeah, we should just sit quietly and look at some books", said Emmet.

"Why don't you try a puzzle book?" suggested Tali, "I have some in the van".

"But, won't someone else have already done all the puzzles?" asked Emmet.

"Yeah, if the books have been borrowed by someone else, they will have completed the crosswords and Word-Searches", added Joe.

"Ah, but these are magic puzzle books" said Tali with a smile, "Try one".

Joe took a puzzle book from the shelf and sat at Tali's desk to complete a crossword. When he had finished it, Tali told him to put it back on the shelf. There was a small flash as the book went back into place but Joe did not notice it.

Tali then told Emmet to take the same book down again. When Emmet opened it, the crossword was blank again!

"That's amazing", said Emmet, "Let's try a dot-to-dot puzzle next".

(In case you don't know, this involves drawing a line between a series of numbered dots to make a picture.)

"I've got a better idea", said Tali and led the boys out of the van.

There, on their front garden were a number of metal pins with numbers on them stuck into the grass. Tali gave the boys a big ball of white string and told them to stretch it between the pins, following the numbers.

They started at number 1 and laid the string between it and number 2 and then 3 and then 4 and so on ...

When they reached number 78, they had run out of string.

From where the boys stood, it just looked like a jumble of string and grass. Tali told them to go upstairs to their bedroom and look at it from the window.

Joe and Emmet ran upstairs excitedly.

When they saw it from above, they could see that the white string on the grassy background formed some words.

Joe read them out and they said:

Are you two boys really ill?

They suddenly remembered that they were pretending to be unwell, so they walked back down the stairs very slowly. Joe even managed to limp a little bit in case his Mummy was watching.

"Let's try a maze puzzle next", cried Joe, "I love finding my way from the start to the finish, tracing a line with a pen through the maze."

Tali twitched his nose and the metal pins and string on the grass making the dot-to-dot puzzle all vanished.

Instead, there in the garden was an actual maze!

It was made from rows of tall hedges which the boys could not see over. Tali gave them a map of the maze with the words 'START' and 'FINISH' marked on it. The 'FINISH' was right in the centre of the maze.

The boys ran excitedly along the rows of the maze.

Joe shouted, "This is a-MAZE-ing" and Emmet laughed at his joke.

They were having great fun and were whooping and cheering as they turned the final corner into the 'FINISH'; and what did they find there? …

… their Mummy, sitting on a chair drinking a cup of tea.

"Hello boys", she said, "you seem to have made a remarkable recovery. I think you'll be well enough for school this afternoon".

"Oh-Oh", said the boys together; they had been caught out!

The two boys went up to their bedroom to get changed into their uniforms, ready for school.

When they came down, the maze had disappeared and Tali was standing by the door of the van.

"You should never try to trick your Mummy. It never works", he told them.   (Very wise, Tali)

A new magnet in the shape of a Word-Search puzzle was attached to the end of his desk and he gave them both a printed copy to do after school.

Here it is:

Can you find the names of all these people who have been mentioned in the stories in this book (so far)?

M	R	S	B	L	A	C	K	Q	L
R	O	M	R	N	F	O	X	O	F
S	S	A	G	E	R	A	R	D	Y
O	I	R	E	I	D	N	A	S	S
H	E	Y	U	G	A	S	Z	P	I
A	M	A	G	N	U	S	Y	I	W
R	M	N	J	G	E	L	Z	R	E
E	E	N	N	O	L	I	F	A	L
P	T	A	L	I	E	G	V	T	Y
M	O	T	L	E	I	B	B	E	D

Angus	Magnus	Lilly	Evie
Sandie	Debbie	Pirate	Mrs O'Hare
Lewis	Lorna	Mrs Black	Tali
Mr N Fox	Gerard	Mary Anna	Guy
Tom	Rosie	Joe	Emmet

(Since these are bedtime stories, perhaps you should do the puzzle in the morning. Goodnight, sleep tight!)

Chapter 15

Poetry Books

One morning, Tali could not stop smiling. He had a huge, wide smile all across his face. He looked in the mirror and saw that his smile was even wider than his whole head.

"What's going on here?" he wondered.

Then he opened his mouth and saw that he had a whole cucumber sideways in there!

Then he woke up!

He had been dreaming!

He saw a plate of crackers and slices of cucumber beside his bed. That had been his supper the night before and he must have continued to think about cucumbers while he was asleep.

(Crazy Bookhound!)

He dreeped down into the van and had his breakfast (not cucumber).

Soon, it was time for the library to open and Tali saw three people waiting outside. They were friends called Patrick, Jen and Logan.

"Good morning, Tali", said Patrick, "we need your help".

"Our teacher has asked us to write a poem", added Jen.

"And we're a bit stuck", said Logan.

"OK", said Tali, "what have you got so far?"

"All we can think of is 'A fat cat sat on a mat'", Patrick replied.

"With a rat on his hat", added Jen.

"... and that's that!" Logan said.

"Well, it certainly rhymes", Tali said, trying not to laugh, "but it needs a bit of work. Have a look in the 'POETRY' section of the library and see what books you can find."

The poetry books were all twitching with excitement as the friends approached; each one wanting to be chosen.

"Choose me, choose me. I'm number 1. I'm sure to bring you lots of fun".

"Choose me, choose me. I'm number 2. I'm sure I'll be just right for you".

"Choose me, choose me. I'm number 3. We'll have a laugh if you choose me".

Finally, they chose a book called:

I'm a Poet – and I Know It

by

Alex Forrest

Logan took it over to Tali's desk and the bookhound put it on the magic stand.

The shelves did their 'spinny' thing and the three friends had to hold on to each other to stop themselves from falling over.

When the door of the van opened, they found themselves at the front door of the **National Poetry Museum.**

They saw a tall man there with a badge which said:

"**Alex Forrest - Poetry Expert**"

This was the man who had written the poetry book which they had chosen in the library!

Jen thought he looked incredibly strong and handsome and could not stop herself from telling him so.

"Oh, the strength comes from carrying poetry books around the museum all day. The handsomeness is from my dad's side of the family", said Alex.

"We Forrests have always been handsome", he added modestly.

Tali was pleased that <u>his</u> books were magic and put themselves away every night. <u>He</u> did not have to carry lots of heavy books around.

"Come away in and I'll show you how to write poems", said Handsome Alex giving a friendly smile to the three friends and a wink to Tali.

In the museum there were various sections, just like in Tali's library-van.

There were sections called:

- LONG BORING POEMS
  - "No thanks", said Logan.
- REALLY, REALLY LONG POEMS
  - "Eh, No", said Jen
- EVEN LONGER, MORE BORING POEMS
  - "Get us out of here!" cried Patrick
- FUNNY POEMS
  - "That sounds better", they all agreed.

Handsome Alex took them to the 'FUNNY POEMS' section and showed them lots of different exhibits. The poems were printed on cards on the walls of the museum.

The first poem was:

- ➢ Soldier Freddy was never ready,
- ➢ But! Soldier Neddy, unlike Freddy, was always ready and steady.
- ➢ That's why, when Soldier Neddy Is-outside-Buckingham-Palace-on-guard-in-the-pouring-wind-and-rain-being-steady-and-ready …
- ➢ … Freddy is home in beddy.

"That rhymes just like our cat-mat-hat-rat poem", said Patrick.

Alex explained that rhyming was not the only important thing about poetry. The rhythm is important too. The rhythm is the beat the words make, like:

- Di-da-di-da-di-da-di-da
- Di-da-di-da-di-da
- Di-da-di-da-di-da-di-da
- Di-da-di-da-di-da

The next poem Alex showed them was:

- On yonder hill there stood a coo.
- It moved away. It's no' there noo.

- There stood a coo on yonder hill.
- It moved away. It's no' there still.

Jen giggled.

(Either at the funny poem or to impress Alex, I'm not quite sure.)

Patrick liked the next poem:

- As I was walking down the stair
- I met a man who wasn't there
- He wasn't there again today
- Oh, how I wish he'd go away.

"Eh? How could you meet him if he wasn't there?" asked Logan.

"These are called 'nonsense rhymes'", explained Alex, "They are just for fun and don't have to make sense. That's why they are called 'non-sense'".

"But the rhythm is good", said Tali, "and here's another poem with a strange rhyme".

- A wonderful bird is the pelican;
- Its beak can hold more than its belly can.

The friends said they were beginning to understand what was needed to write a poem. They went back into the library-van after Jen had given Mr Forrest an unnecessarily-long hug.

When Esmerelda returned them home, Tali gave them special books to help with their poetry project.

"But these are full of blank pages", said Jen.

"Exactly: that's the best type of book; one which leaves you free to fill it with your own ideas", said Tali, "Now, write me a poem".

The three friends got together and came up with this:

(See if you can guess the rhyming word at the end of each verse)

- ❖ Tali is a bookhound who lives inside a van.
- ❖ And when we want to borrow books, he helps us if he …
  - ✓ … can.
- ❖ He sleeps up in the roof-space and dreeps down every day.
- ❖ He dreeps because the pile of books have put themselves …
  - ✓ … away.
- ❖ When we tell the bookhound which books we'd like to find,
- ❖ He always tries to help because he's very, very …
  - ✓ … kind.
- ❖ The stand on Tali's desk holds the book which we have found.
- ❖ We set off on adventures when the shelves all spin …
  - ✓ … around.
- ❖ We all have fun and learn a lot with Tali as our friend.
- ❖ He brings us safely back again. Our poem's done. **THE** …
  - ✓ … **END**.

Tali was very proud of their poem and said that their teacher would be pleased.

Before the three friends left for home they gave Tali a new magnet. It was in the shape of a book with no writing in it.

"That's to remind people that the best type of book is one where you add your own ideas", said Patrick.

"Thanks very much", said Tali and he then started to prepare his supper for bedtime.

He made sure there was no cucumber this time!

Chapter 16

Sci-Fi Books

Next morning, Tali checked the mirror to make sure he did not have a big, wide smile. He just had his usual, nice smile.

When the library opened, his first customers were a man called Mike and his daughter, Julie.

Mike said that he was a big fan of Science Fiction books (or Sci-Fi for short). He wanted to introduce Julie to some of these stories but she was a bit scared of the space monsters which usually appear in them.

Mike comforted her and told her not to be scared. "They're only made-up stories", he said, "That's why they're called Science <u>Fiction</u>. Fiction means that it's not real".

Julie was still a bit wary but she had a look on the shelves and eventually chose a book with a picture of the Moon on it.

She liked how the craters on the moon looked like a smiling face.

"That's why people call it 'the Man on the Moon'", said Tali.

"I'd love to visit 'the Man on the Moon' out in space", she sighed.

"Then, let's see what we can do", said the bookhound.

He placed her chosen book on the special stand on his desk and the library-van's door closed. As the shelves started spinning round, Mike got a fright and shouted: "Help! What's going on!"

Now it was Julie's turn to comfort her dad.

"Just hold my hand and you'll be fine", she told him, winking at Tali.

When the spinning stopped and the door opened, Esmerelda was parked beside the biggest crater on the Moon!

Mike, Julie and Tali all went outside and were amazed at what they saw. They could see the Earth nearby and the Sun shining in the distance.

Suddenly, Julie saw a baddie's spaceship flying between the Earth and the Moon. She knew it was a baddie's ship because it had:

'Baddies are Good'

written on the side of it.

As it approached the Sun, a big, robotic arm came out of the top of the spaceship. The arm was holding a massive watering-can and it poured water all over the Sun and put it out!

It immediately got very dark and cold on the Moon and Tali had to use a firefly torch to guide Julie and Mike back to Esmerelda.

Once inside, Tali quickly closed the door and they all headed back to Earth.

Back home, it was freezing because there was no sunshine to keep everything warm and cosy.

All the rivers had turned to ice and penguins were skating on the duck-ponds.

The ducks were all wearing woolly hats and scarves and polar bears were sitting around on deck-chairs, wearing sunglasses.

They did not really need to wear these since there was no sun but they thought the glasses made them look cool.

"How can we re-light the Sun?" asked Julie, getting worried.

"I have an idea", said Mike. He stood on the roof of Esmerelda and took out the lighter he used to light candles for Julie's birthday cake. He stretched up as far as he could but he was nowhere near the Sun.

Next, Tali got all of his friends to light barbecues in their gardens, hoping that the heat from all of the fires would somehow set fire to the soggy Sun. But, no luck.

The smell of all the sausages and burgers and chicken legs made the Man on the Moon lick his lips and feel very hungry. He was enjoying the smell so much that he took a very deep breath.

He breathed in a lot of the barbecue smoke!

It made him cough a lot and then he did a massive sneeze ..

Aaaaaaaachhhoooooo

His massive sneeze travelled through space and blew out all of the barbecues down on Earth.

Tali, Julie and Mike were all huddled inside Esmerelda trying to keep warm when, suddenly, Julie noticed one of the magnets on Tali's desk.

She saw the green dragon on the carousel and asked Tali about it.

"That's my friend, Debbie the Dragon. Wait a minute! You've just given me a great idea!" he shouted.

Tali contacted Debbie and asked for her help.

She flew in with a big lump of burning lava from a volcano and Tali used it to warm himself and his friends. Debbie said that she had just eaten some very hot lava for her dinner and her breath was still very fiery.

She flew off into space and breathed fire at the Sun.

It burst into flames and the Earth was suddenly light and warm again.

Debbie chased the baddie and his spaceship off into outer space and he was never seen again.

When Debbie got back to Earth, everyone was cheering … except for the polar bears and penguins.

They were annoyed because they had to go back to their own homes at the North and South Poles to keep cool.

Just wearing sunglasses is not cool enough for most polar bears; they need ice and snow.

Mike and Julie were feeling a bit warmer and thanked Tali for their exciting day of Science Fiction.

When he got home, Tali noticed two new magnets on his desk.

One magnet was a sun …

… the other was a watering-can.

Tali made sure to keep them as far apart as possible.

He did not want the Sun to go out again!

Chapter 17

Bird Books

One snowy, winter's morning, Tali was having his breakfast in the van which was parked in Cramond.

He sat at his desk eating a toasted bagel with some of his Granny Lorna's homemade strawberry jam spread on it.

He was just about to take a bite when, suddenly, a little, brown bird flew in the window, pecked a bit of the bagel in Tali's hand and flew back out of the window.

Tali was very surprised; he had never been so close to a wild bird before.

He was happy to share a bit of his bagel as he had nearly eaten one half and still had the other half to eat. He was planning to spread some of his Granny's raspberry jam on this other bit.

He was just opening the jam jar when a big black and white bird flew in the open window, picked up all of the remaining bagel and zoomed back out the window with it in its beak.

"Hey!" shouted Tali as he sped out of Esmerelda's door, "That's my breakfast!"

It was very cold outside, so Tali went back in to fetch a scarf and gloves. He also put on a woolly hat which his Granny had knitted for him. It had lots of different colours and a big pom-pom on the top.

(His Granny is very clever, making jam and hats, isn't she?)

Outside on the snow-covered ground, there was a group of birds all munching away at his breakfast!

The birds were called:

- Jenny Wren
- Jack Daw
- Robin Redbreast
- Maggie Pie
- Polly Parrot

(Isn't it funny how we give birds boys' and girls' names? Do you know which bird is which?)

Tali told the hungry birds, "I don't mind sharing my breakfast with you but you can't have it all. You must leave <u>me</u> something".

"Sorry", said Jack Daw, "but we are all starving. We can't get any of our usual food because it's all covered with snow".

"And, another thing", said Maggie Pie, "we usually drink from the bird-bath or puddles but we can't get any water since it's all frozen".

Tali looked around and saw that two cheeky squirrels wearing ice-skates were skating on the ice on the top of the bird-bath.

Tali felt sorry for the birds and said that they could keep his bagel. He was lucky and had lots of other things which he could have for his breakfast.

(What kind of things do you like to have for breakfast?)

Tali went back into the library-van and picked up a big hammer from his tool box. He went over to the bird-bath and smashed the ice. The two squirrels fell into the water and got soaking wet. They were NOT pleased.

"Serves you right", said Robin Redbreast as he took a big drink of water.

Tali returned to Esmerelda and sat at his desk. He was worried about the birds not having any food. He wanted to help them but realised that he did not know what birds like to eat. He was wondering how he could find that out.

(How do you think Tali could find out what kind of things birds like to eat?)

He was still sitting at his desk when he heard a voice saying:

"Ahem, excuse me, over here!"

Tali looked over and saw that a book had sprouted wings and was flying around the 'NATURE' section of the library, like a bird. He jumped up and caught the book and saw that it was called:

Garden Birds

The book's wings folded away as Tali took it back to his desk. The book told him where each type of bird builds its nest and what they like to eat.

They mostly like nuts and seeds and suet-balls.

Tali bought some of these from a shop and put them out on the snow for the birds to eat.

The two naughty squirrels came running over and started to eat all of the bird food. Tali had to chase them away. He put some nuts and suet-balls into wire feeder cages and hung them from the roof of the library-van. The birds could fly up and get the food but the squirrels could not reach them.

The next morning Tali drove Esmerelda to Newhaven along the river and then he realised his mistake. The nuts were still attached to the van and so there would be no food for Jenny Wren and her friends.

He immediately drove back to Cramond.

The birds were all sitting in a row on a telephone wire, hungry.

"Oopsee", said Tali, "Sorry for taking the bird food away with me". He took the feeder cages off Esmerelda's roof and tied them to a tree. The birds all flocked to them and started pecking at the nuts and suet.

Then he said goodbye to the birds and set off in Esmerelda heading for Newhaven again, leaving the bird-feeders full of yummy bird food tied to the tree.

But ...

... the next time Tali came back to Cramond, the birds were all sitting on the telephone wire again. The bird-feeders were empty!

"What happened to all the nuts and suet-balls?" he asked.

Polly Parrot replied, "It's those squirrels again. They climbed up the tree, ran along the branch and helped themselves to all of the nuts!"

Quick as a flash, Tali got a bottle of the bubble-mix he keeps in the van for blowing bubbles at parties. He poured the soapy mixture along the branch of the tree.

Tali put new nuts into the feeders and then he and the birds all hid inside Esmerelda and peeked out of the window to see what happened next.

The two naughty squirrels ran up the tree trunk but when they tried to run along the branch to get the nuts, they slipped on the bubble-mix and fell out of the tree.

One landed in a muddy puddle.

The other landed in the bird-bath; so they both got soaked again!

Tali and the birds all laughed as the wet squirrels ran away, dripping wet.

He thought they would have learned not to steal the birds' food again but, just to make sure, he changed the feeders for some extra wide ones.

These allowed the birds to fly in and get to the nuts but stopped the squirrels from reaching the yummy food.

Tali was pleased to have helped his feathered friends and they gave him a 'thank you' present.

(Can you guess what it was?)

It was a magnet in the shape of a bagel.

Robin Redbreast had stuck some of his red feathers onto it to make it look like it had raspberry jam on it …

… just like the bagel which the birds had stolen from Tali's breakfast table.

So, if you ever see a row of birds sitting on a telephone wire, it could mean that Tali will soon be there to fill up the bird-feeders.

Or perhaps <u>you</u> could put some food and water out for the birds yourself, in case Tali is late.

Chapter 18

Vehicle Repair Books

Gerard Supercat came to see Tali at the library-van one day. Well, no-one knew it was Gerard Supercat since he did not have his disguise on. All anyone could see was Gerard Cat arriving on his bike.

Gerard had grown too big for his scooter and now used a bike with stabilisers on it.

When he arrived, Esmerelda was all locked up; the library was not open.

The curtains on Tali's bedroom-tent were still closed too. Very strange.

Gerard banged on the door and shouted to Tali.

"What's going on? Why is the library closed?"

Suddenly, a piece of paper landed at Gerard's feet. When he unfolded it, there was a key wrapped inside. The paper had writing on it. It said:

"I'm ill in bed. Here's the key to the van. Let yourself in and the books will help you to find what you need. Cough, Cough."

(I think Tali added that last bit so that Gerard would feel sorry for him!)

Gerard opened the door and went inside. He told the books that he was looking for instructions about how to remove the stabilisers from his bike and how to make the saddle a bit higher.

Suddenly, a book in the 'VEHICLE MAINTENANCE' section of the library started to nudge its way forward on the shelf. It fell out and landed on Gerard's foot.

"AYAH", he shouted but soon forgot the pain when he saw that it was called:

Bicycle Repairs for Cats

"Just exactly what I'm looking for", thought Gerard as he took it over to Tali's desk. He looked at all the instructions about how to mend flat tyres, put oil on the chain and all the other repairs he wanted to do to his bike.

Suddenly, Gerard realised that he had never been in the library-van on his own before; Tali had always been with him. He started to have a look around.

He tried to open the top-left drawer of the desk (the one which magicked up the books for Tali) but it was shut tight. Then he noticed the driving seat in the van.

"I've never sat up there before", he said to himself, "I wonder what it's like".

He jumped up onto the seat and started playing with the steering wheel and all the controls which Tali uses to drive Esmeralda from town to town. He pressed a lever and the window-wipers came on. He watched them swishing back and forward until he felt a bit dizzy.

Then Gerard found the 'horn' button and pressed it. Esmerelda's horn made a noise like:

'Cough, Cough!'

When Tali was ill, Esmerelda always felt unwell too!

Gerard managed to start the engine and decided he would like to drive the library-van. He had never driven a van or a car before; only scooters and bikes (with stabilisers).

He drove down a road which had a very low bridge over it. Esmerelda could fit under the bridge but Tali's bedroom tent was too tall. The tent was going to hit the bridge!

Gerard did not know this as he sped down the road getting faster and faster!

Just before they reached the bridge, Esmerelda did some magic. She lowered Tali's bedroom down into the library. It just missed the stone bridge by two inches!

Tali slept all the way through this.

By this time, Gerard was driving so fast that the van was swerving about all over the place. It nearly toppled over as Gerard turned a corner at great speed.

Suddenly, some big metal bars with wheels attached to them shot out from the sides of the library-van.

Esmerelda had put out stabilisers to keep herself from falling over!

Gerard had completely lost control now and the van crashed through a fence and into a field. Esmerelda came to a halt in the middle of a big puddle of mud.

"Oh-Oh! Now I'm in trouble", said Gerard but, luckily, Tali was still asleep.

Gerard promised Esmerelda that he would drive more slowly and so she retracted her stabilisers and let him reverse out of the field.

He thought it would be a good idea to go through a car-wash to get all the mud off the van. He drove up to the machine and paid the man some money before driving into the car-wash. The bedroom-tent was still down in the library so Esmerelda just fitted in. Gerard switched off the engine and let the van be pulled along through all the brushes and hoses.

As soon as the machine started up, Gerard realised that he had not put the window back up after paying. The water was gushing in and soaking him.

By the time be got the window back up, there was a huge puddle on the floor of the library. The rubber duck magnet from Tali's desk was swimming about in it!

"Oh-Oh! Now I really am in trouble", said Gerard, but the books came to the rescue. They started their spinning around and the door of the van flew open. Just like the spin-drier you sometimes get at swimming pools to dry your costume, all the water poured out of the door.

Gerard grabbed the duck magnet and stuck it back on Tali's desk. He hoped it was in the right place or Tali would know something was wrong.

With all the mud washed off the van, Gerard noticed that there were some big scratches on Esmerelda's paintwork!

He looked on the shelves and found another book called:

Paintwork Repairs for Library-Vans

(Tali's library has books for every problem, doesn't it?)

This book told him that you can cover the scratches with paint using a brush or a spray-gun. Gerard did not have any paint with him (he had not brought his Supercat tool-bag) so he looked in Tali's cupboard.

He saw a tin of mushy-peas.

"They're green, the same colour as the library-van's paint", he thought, "That will do!"

He did not have a brush either so he borrowed Tali's toothbrush.

Luckily, Tali was <u>still</u> asleep and did not know what Gerard was up to!

Gerard tried brushing the peas over the scratches but it was not very easy.

He decided to try another method which he had seen in the Paintwork Repair Book.

This method used a spray-gun!

Gerard had to add some water to the mushy-peas to make them more sloppy then he poured the sloppy-mushy-peas into a water-pistol.

(Gerard always has a water-pistol with him.)

He was just finishing squirting the green mess all over the front of the van when he heard Tali dreeping down into the library. Tali was surprised that he did not have so far to dreep as his bedroom was in the van. He came out of the door and said:

"Hi Gerard. Here's a funny thing... I've just brushed my teeth and there's a funny taste ... a bit like mushy-peas! And why are those sheep licking the front of the library-van?"

Sure enough, some sheep had come over and were licking all the sloppy-mushy-pea-paint from Esmerelda. Tali could now see all the scratches on her paintwork and asked Gerard:

"What's been going on while I was asleep?"

Gerard had to tell Tali all that had happened and said he'd pay to have the scratches painted over properly ... and for a tin of mushy-peas ... and a new toothbrush.

Esmerelda raised Tali's bed back up onto the roof and Gerard said he was sorry for the crazy driving he had done.

Gerard decided that he would give Esmerelda a present too.

It was a magnet with a picture of herself on it.

On the magnet, her door was open and you could see Tali's desk.

On the side of the desk in the picture was a magnet with Esmeralda with her door open and you could see Tali's desk ....

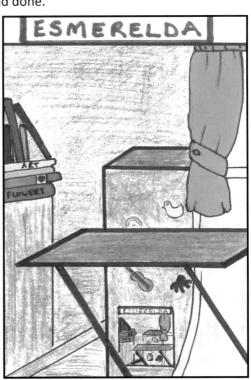

Chapter 19

Drama Books – Act 1

Tali was having another weird dream.

He dreamt that he was at the theatre watching a show. Suddenly it seemed to be snowing inside the theatre. Everyone in the audience was covered with white snow!

Even after he had woken up, Tali kept thinking about his theatre dream.

He could not work it out.

When Tali was not working in the library-van, he often liked to go to the theatre to see plays. His weird dream made him think that he would like to put on a play himself (with his friends, of course!)

He wondered how he could let his friends know about his plans for the play and then he remembered that he had seen noticeboards in other libraries advertising coffee-mornings, Lego-clubs and colouring-in-clubs (for adults!!)

Tali decided to put up a notice on the side of Esmerelda.

It said:

Tali's Drama Club – All Welcome

Meet here at 5 o'clock each Monday

Tali wasn't sure if anyone would be interested in helping him to put on a play but he hoped that someone would.

He should not have worried because the following Monday night, when Tali opened the door of the van, there was a big crowd of people waiting.

Amongst them, he saw:

- Trevor (the rabbit with three ears),
- Declan (his friend, the rabbit with ten ears),
- Martha (the magical mouse),
- Mary (her friend the musical mouse),
- Misha and Gerard (the Supercats)
- Mrs O'Hare and a lot of the Dancing Rabbit Chorus
- Mr N Fox ("Oh-Oh! I'd better keep a close eye on him. He's very naughty", thought Tali to himself.)

"Welcome everybody", said Tali, "I'm sure we will make a splendid Drama Club".

Everyone cheered and clapped then the fox said, "I don't really know what a Drama Club is. Everyone else seemed to be coming this way so I just followed them". A few other people nodded and said they were not sure what it was either.

"It's where people get together to put on a play", he told them.

"Oh, I'm not sure that I want to be up on a stage", said Mrs O'Hare.

"You don't <u>have</u> to be on the stage", Tali replied, "In a Drama Club, some people act, some people make the costumes and others sell tickets and ice-creams. There's always something for everyone to do".

Several people decided to join the club and Tali said he thought it would be a good idea if they all went to see a stage show to let them see what happens. Tali always keeps some newspapers and magazines in the library-van so he looked in the local paper to see what shows were currently on nearby.

As soon as he opened the paper, a flyer for a play came flying out and fluttered about in the air in front of his face.

(Maybe that's why they're called 'flyers'?)

It was for a show called *'Brave Macbeth'* which was based on a play by William Shakespeare. Tali thought that Esmerelda was trying to tell him that this was a good show, so he decided that they should go to see it.

When they arrived at the theatre, it was quite busy. As you may know, Trevor and Declan always like to sit in the back row so that their ears do not block anyone's view.

Sadly, all the seats in the back row were full.

There were two seats empty at the end of a row near the front and the multi-eared rabbits headed for them. Declan sat down and then, just as Trevor was about to sit beside him, the fox nipped in and took his seat.

"Hey! I was going to sit there!" said Trevor, "Oh, never mind, I'll sit here", and he took the seat behind Declan.

They soon found that the theatre seats all had strong springs on them. When no-one was sitting on them they bounced upright. You had to push hard to flip them down to sit on them.

Declan had bought some of his favourite carrot ice-cream and after he sat down, he put the tub on the front corner of his seat.

Suddenly, a lady needed to go out to the toilet, so they all had to stand up to let her pass.

As soon as Declan stood up, his seat bounced up again.

The ice-cream tub flew up in the air and landed on Trevor's face in the row behind!

Everyone thought it was very funny, except Trevor, of course. He tried to throw the ice-cream tub back at Declan.

The fox next to Declan was so busy laughing at Trevor that he did not notice that his seat had flipped up too. When he sat back down again, he fell right onto the floor!

The fox stood up again just as Trevor threw the ice-cream tub and it hit him on the head.

He grabbed it and squashed it into Declan's face.

Now, all three of them had carrot ice-cream on their faces.

Trevor and Declan loved carrot ice-cream and so were happy to eat-up all the splashes.

The fox said that he preferred chicken-flavoured ice-cream … (*yuk.*)

After a few minutes, the show started so everyone sat down quickly.

The play was great! Everyone enjoyed the story and the singing and dancing that went with it.

It was also very funny.

Every time someone was stabbed with a sword (under their arm, not for real) they made a funny squeaking sound and fell onto the floor.

As well as enjoying the play, Tali reminded them that they were also there to learn how to put on a show so everyone watched carefully to see how all the different people in the theatre worked together.

After the show, Tali had arranged for them to meet the director of the play, a very kind and clever man called Nick Hayes.

Nick was very keen on music and drama and had spent many years helping young people to make the most of their performing talents.

He said he was very excited about Tali's Drama Club and said he was sure that their play would be a great success.

Everyone was looking forward to the next Monday when they could start work on their own play.

Tali was still thinking about his weird dream and wondered if snow would be a part of their show.

We'll find out next time what happened when they started work on it.

(I have a funny feeling that it might not go according to plan, don't you?)

Chapter 20

Drama Books – Act 2

Tali thought that the visit to the theatre had been a great success (at least it didn't snow) and everyone was keen to start working on their own play.

Tali had chosen a book of plays from the 'DRAMA' section of the library.

Each play has a set of instructions about what each of the actors should say. It also tells you when to open and shut the curtains and when the lights should go on and off.

These instructions are called a 'script'.

Just like *'Brave Macbeth'*, the play which Tali chose had music, singing and dancing in it (and no snow). It was a 'musical' play about a fierce dragon who lived in a windmill. All the people in the village were scared of the dragon so they sent a handsome prince up to the windmill to fight it.

Tali gave a copy of the script to everyone who was involved so they all knew what they were supposed to do and say.

The actors had to learn their lines and try to remember them because they would not be allowed to have their scripts with them during the performance of the play.

Here are all the roles the various people were going to play:

- Director – **Tali Bookhound**
    - The director is the boss and tells everyone what to do.
- The Dragon – **Debbie the Dragon**
    - The sly fox wanted to play the part of the dragon, but Tali thought that Debbie would be better since she's actually a dragon. She was delighted to join the Drama Club.
- The Handsome Price – **Trevor**
    - In the play, he comes to fight the dragon with a wooden sword which Gerard made with his tools.
- The Windmill - **Declan**
    - He has to stand on the stage and stick his ten ears out like the sails of a windmill.
- Sound Effects, Lighting and Curtains – **Martha Mouse**
    - She has to magic up thunder and lightning from behind the scenery so that no-one knows that she is magical. She also produces wind to make the windmill turn.
- Ticket and Ice-cream Sales – **Misha and Gerard, the Supercats**
    - They had to fly all over the place asking people to buy tickets for the play. They will also sell ice-cream to the audience on the night of the show.
- Music – **Mary Mouse**
    - She used a lot of homemade instruments to make the music for the show. She made a recording of the music and planned to play it during the performance so that she does not miss seeing the play herself.
- The Villagers – **Mrs O'Hare and the Dancing Rabbit Chorus**
    - They had to stand at the side of the stage and sing songs to make the prince feel brave as he tackled the dragon.

- Costumes, Props and Stage Management – **Mr N Fox**
  - His job was to make sure Trevor had his sword with him and that all the rabbits in the chorus had the correct clothes on. At the end of the play he was supposed to throw flowers onto the stage to thank the actors for their great performances.

Once everyone agreed to these jobs, Tali made up flyers and posters to advertise the show.

The Supercats took them all over town and asked people to put them in shop windows so that everyone would know where and when they could see the show.

During the rehearsals, Trevor took off one of his ears because he thought a prince should only have two ears. This meant he could not hear properly and missed his cue when it was his time to speak.

Tali got annoyed with Trevor and asked the fox to give 'the prince' a fancy feather hat to wear. This meant that Trevor could hide his third ear under the hat and be able to hear properly.

Everyone was happy; Trevor knew when it was his turn to speak and they continued with their rehearsal.

After a while, and lots of practising, Tali thought that they were ready for the big night.

They were all a bit nervous but Tali held up his script and said:

"It's all in here, my friends. Just follow the script. What can go wrong?"

(Well, let's see what can go wrong!) ....

The show started well.

The audience took their seats after buying programmes and ice-creams from Gerard and Misha.

Declan stuck his ten ears out to make a magnificent windmill and Mary pretended to conduct the orchestra with a wooden spoon from the space in front of the stage (remember she had made a recording of the music).

Everything was going perfectly until the prince started fighting the dragon.

Debbie breathed out fire and set Trevor's wooden sword alight.

He ran about with a flaming sworn and the audience laughed. He finally plunged the burning sword into a bucket of water at the side of the stage.

There was a loud 'HISSSSSSSS' as the water put out the flames.

Trevor came back onto the stage with a new, metal sword, which just glowed brightly when Debbie's fiery breath touched it. This sword did NOT catch fire!

At the end of their battle, he is supposed to put out the Dragon's flame with water, but his old sword was still in the water bucket.

He saw another bucket next to it and used that instead.

Sadly, this bucket was full of bubble-mixture for the party after the show. Trevor did not know this and poured it over Debbie.

She coughed and spluttered and suddenly there were hundreds of bubbles filled with smoke all over the stage.

The dancing rabbits could not see where they were going because of all the smoke and slipped on the bubbles.

They all ended up in a big 'pile-on' in the middle of the stage.

The audience thought this is meant to happen and they laughed and laughed until their sides were sore.

Tali did not mind at all because he knew that everyone was trying hard.

He was pleased to see them all having such a good time.

It really was quite a funny show.

(Can you name all the characters in the picture on the next page?)

Finally, the play ended and the actors lined up along the front of the stage.

The fox was supposed to throw the flowers for them to catch. He had not listened properly and heard 'flour' instead of 'flowers'.

He chucked a big bag of baking flour all over the actors!

This made Declan, the Windmill, sneeze and he blew the flour out from the stage. The whole audience was covered in white dust but they just kept on laughing.

Tali realised that this was just like in his dream. The 'snow' he had seen was actually flour!

The audience joined in with all the actors and they enjoyed a huge 'flour' fight. They threw handfuls of flour, like snowballs, at each other. It was great fun but it made a terrible mess.

(I'm sure Martha would find some way of tidying up all the mess in the theatre. What magic spell do you think she could use?)

Instead of getting a magnet to remind him of the show, Tali pasted hundreds of flyers to the walls of his bedroom on top of Esmerelda.

He also stuck up the label from the bag of flour.

This meant that, every morning when he woke up, he would remember the fun he had putting on a play with all his friends and the 'snow storm' at the end of the show.

(Would you like to put on a play with your friends?)

Word-Search Solution

Here is the answer to the WordSearch puzzle from chapter 14.

M	R	S	B	L	A	C	K	Q	L
R	O	M	R	N	F	O	X	O	F
S	S	A	G	E	R	A	R	D	Y
O	I	R	E	I	D	N	A	S	S
H	E	Y	U	G	A	S	Z	P	I
A	M	A	G	N	U	S	Y	I	W
R	M	N	J	G	E	L	Z	R	E
E	E	N	N	O	L	I	F	A	L
P	T	A	L	I	E	G	V	T	Y
M	O	T	L	E	I	B	B	E	D

Angus	Magnus	Lilly	Evie
Sandie	Debbie	Pirate	Mrs O'Hare
Lewis	Lorna	Mrs Black	Tali
Mr N Fox	Gerard	Mary-Anna	Guy
Tom	Rosie	Joe	Emmet

More Bedtime Stories

The Rabbit with Three Ears

The Rabbit with Three Ears gets up to tricks with other rabbits, pigeons, a seagull, a fox, a dog, a mole and a cat.

Martha, the Magical Mouse

Martha the Mouse discovers that she can do magical things (sometimes).

She and her musical friend, Mary, have lots of adventures in London and elsewhere.

She visits her cousin Trevor, the Rabbit with Three Ears, during the Edinburgh Festival and they all take a camping trip to the island of Arran.

Misha looks like an ordinary pet cat but she is really a superhero.

She and her side-kick Gerard rescue and advise people in need all over Edinburgh.

Gerard is a really clumsy cat but he tries to copy Misha as they perform their various missions.

He dreams of becoming a real superhero too.

Printed in Poland
by Amazon Fulfillment
Poland Sp. z o.o., Wrocław

50152003R00072